E. L. Anderson

Soldier and Pioneer

A biographical Sketch of Lt.-Col Richard C. Anderson

E. L. Anderson

Soldier and Pioneer
A biographical Sketch of Lt.-Col Richard C. Anderson

ISBN/EAN: 9783337137083

Printed in Europe, USA, Canada, Australia, Japan

Cover: Foto ©Raphael Reischuk / pixelio.de

More available books at **www.hansebooks.com**

SOLDIER AND PIONEER:

A BIOGRAPHICAL SKETCH OF

Lt.-Col. Richard C. Anderson

OF THE

CONTINENTAL ARMY.

• By E. L. ANDERSON.

NEW YORK:
G. P. PUTNAM'S SONS,
182 Fifth Avenue,
1879.

"BUT SINCE IT PLEASED A VANISH'D EYE,

I GO TO PLANT IT ON HIS TOMB,

THAT IF IT CAN IT THERE MAY BLOOM,

OR DYING, THERE AT LEAST MAY DIE."

IN MEMORIAM.

Contents.

Old Virginia.

IN the latter part of the seventeenth century Robert Anderson came to America from Scotland and purchased an estate, called Goldmines, from the fact that some earlier colonist had there made search for the precious metal, in what is now Hanover county, Virginia.

His son Robert, born January 1, 1712, succeeded him in the possession of the property, and was known, and is now remembered, as "Anderson of Goldmines."

My grandfather, Richard Clough Anderson, of whose life I propose to give

some account, was the fifth child of this
second Robert and Elizabeth, daughter
of Richard Clough, a colonist from
Wales.

The house built by the first Robert,
with massive timbers and great outside
chimneys, still stands, marking the birth-
place of two generations of his descend-
ants. Rocky Mills, formerly the home
of Colonel John Syme, lies upon the one
hand, and upon the other is the once
magnificent plantation of the Dabneys.

From one who, for more than half a
century, has been the owner of Goldmines, I have learned some of the tra-
ditions that are still current concerning
the second Robert. He was, it seems, a
mighty hunter, and delighted in the
company of his neighbor, John Findley,
when following the chase. If, upon ris-
ing in the morning, the day proved favorable to sport, he would stand at his

door, and, by his unaided voice, summon Findley from his house, which lay a full mile off as the crow flies. According to another story, he directed, upon the death of his wife, in November, 1779, that two coffins should be brought from Richmond, for he desired to save his surviving friends the tedious journey over miserable roads, when, in the course of events, a period of seventeen years, as it happened, he should require one. I recollect hearing that Colonel Richard Anderson told how he came unexpectedly upon this *memento mori* when he returned from the wars, and found it in use as a fruit-bin.

My grandfather was born upon the twelfth day of January, 1750. He inherited from his father a love for field sports that characterized him throughout his life. Schools were not always at hand in early Virginia, and the education of the chil-

dren, with many other domestic duties that
are unknown in our economy, fell to the
part of the women of the household. But
it was not often that young Richard could
be brought to his books. While his sis-
ters were caring for the poultry or weav-
ing the threads gathered from the silk-
worms (one of them presented General
Washington with a suit of silk made on
the home loom), he was getting an exact
knowledge of the country for many miles
around, and acquiring a physical endur-
ance almost equal to that of the wild ani-
mals he followed.

At the time of my grandfather's birth,
the white population of the colony did
not exceed one hundred thousand souls.
But little was known of the region that
lay beyond the Blue Ridge mountains,
and what we now reverently style " Old
Virginia," was a sparsely-settled district
abounding in all kinds of game, and not

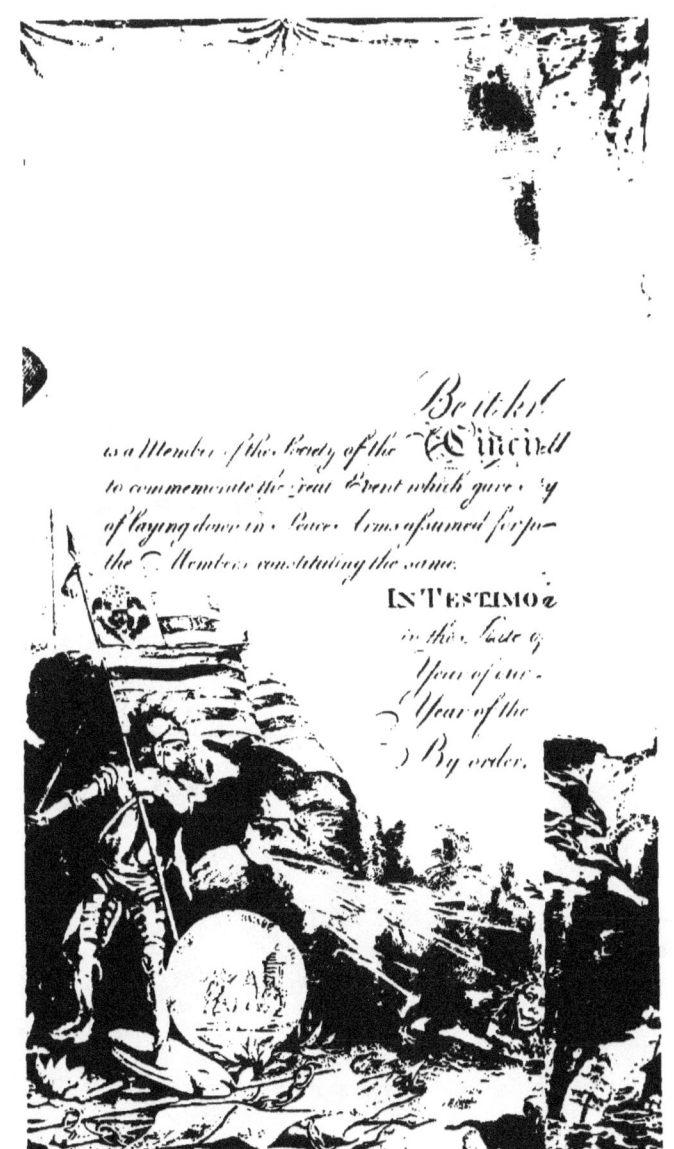

Be it known that **RICHARD CLOUGH ANDERSON** Esq.' Lieu.' Colonel

is a Member of the Society of the *Cincinnati*, instituted by the Officers of the American Army, at the Period of its Dissolution, as well to commemorate th.' great Event which gave Independence to *North America*, as for the laudable Purpose of inculcating the Duty of laying down in Peace Arms assumed for public Defence, and of forming an lasting of Brotherly Affection and Bonds of perpetual Friendship, the Members constituting the same.

IN TESTIMONY whereof I the President of the said Society have hereunto set my Hand at *Philadelphia* in the State of *Pennsylvania* this 19 W.' H .' Year of our Lord One thousand seven Hundred and Eighty four, and in the Eight Year of the Independence of the United States.

By order.

Knox Secretary.   President.

yet free from the dangers of Indian fo-
rays. The negro slaves, amounting in
number to the white colonists, cultivated
tobacco under the direction of overseers,
while the planters employed their time
in attending horse races and cock fights,
or in the more healthy excitement of the
chase.

Richard Anderson was not destined to
be a mere hunter, for Patrick Coots,
who, in wealth and ability, stood at the
head of the merchants of Virginia,
formed so favorable an opinion of him
that he offered to put him in the way of
making his fortune. Anderson of Goldmines did not have the grace to conceal
that it was the contempt he felt for trade
that induced him to oppose this favorable offer; but, in the face of his father's
protest, and against the wishes of all the
family, Richard, at the age of sixteen,
entered the family of the merchant.

Robert Anderson never fully forgave his son for this disobedience, and my grand-father always felt his unjust displeasure.

While Robert Anderson and his neighbors were chasing the fox, and while their daughters, in their frequent interchange of visits, were discussing the latest scandals and fashions from London, for now three hundred ships were employed in carrying out tobacco and introducing foreign follies, young Richard was making voyages as supercargo for the rich merchant, during one of which he saw the tea thrown over into Boston Harbor, an act that did not, perhaps, make any great impression on his mind at the time, but which often recurred to him in after life.

That Richard Anderson retained the good will of Mr. Coots can not be doubted, for when the colonies rose in arms against the mother country, and

Richard joined with the rebels, the loyalist merchant could not bear malice against his young friend, and, on his death-bed, bequeathed him a legacy in proof of his continued affection.

Captain in the Fifth Virginia.

PATRICK HENRY, who was a familiar visitor at the house of Coots, pressed Richard Anderson to accept the position of paymaster-general to the forces that Virginia had offered for the defense of the Colonies. But, upon Anderson expressing a preference for the active service of the line, he was, upon the twenty-sixth day of January, 1776, appointed captain of the company of regulars from Hanover county, and upon the seventh of March following, he received his commission to that grade in the Fifth Virginia Continentals, of which Peachey

(14)

was the colonel, and William Crawford, who perished so miserably by torture in the Indian wars, was the lieutenant-colonel.

My grandfather, at his entrance upon military life, was twenty-six years of age, with mind and body well adapted to the dangers and hardships of a soldier's duties. He was below the medium height, but had broad shoulders and heavily muscled limbs, and, among a race of hardy pioneers, was remarkable for his strength and activity. His face had a lively, and, notwithstanding a nose of disproportionate size, an agreeable expression. He was of cheerful disposition, and exhibited his pleasure by the sparkling of a pair of blue eyes, for he seldom or never laughed. He was fond of society, and talked well, a certain grim humor giving tone to his conversation. I have been told by those who knew him that he was inferior to no man in cool courage, and that he was often selected by his commanding officers for the performance of duties where his judgment and discretion should supply the place of explicit orders. Hugh Pleasants, writing in the *Richmond Despatch*, January 21, 1861, says of him : "There was no braver officer in the American army."

An anecdote that was told of him illustrates very well some of his peculiarities. It seems that Captain Anderson, while standing upon a narrow bridge, overheard some young ladies who were about to pass, commenting upon the size of his nose. With perfect composure, he raised his hat from his head with one hand, and, with the other, turned aside the offending member as though it had been a projecting bough, and desired them to pass. A gentleman of the party, who laughed at the absurdity of the scene, appeased the captain's wrath by an apology.

Colonel Peachey resigned his commission before the regiment took the field, and the Fifth Virginia joined Washington, then about to undertake the movements that culminated in the battle of White Plains, under the command of Colonel Scott, one of the best officers in the Continental army.

The part that Captain Anderson took in the battle of Trenton, in which his regiment was next engaged, merits a particular description, as the relation of it will bring to light certain facts, historically important, that have never been properly represented.

The Battle of Trenton.

UPON the twenty-fourth day of December, 1776, the troops then being encamped near Trenton Falls, Captain Anderson was directed by General Stephen, who had been colonel of the Fourth Virginia Infantry, to cross the Delaware in boats with his company, and, after making a *reconnoissance* in certain directions to return by the way of Trenton, where he should feel for the pickets of the enemy, but avoid engaging a superior force.

At eight o'clock the next evening, Captain Anderson, having so far accom-

(18)

plished his purpose, approached the Hessian outpost at Trenton. A wintry storm was raging, and the sentinel walked his beat with his head turned from the biting hail, unconscious of the approach of the hostile party with their snow muffled feet. The rifle shot that carried his death roused the relief, who rushed from the guard-house to be driven back into the camp. The alarm was soon carried into Trenton, and the troops made ready for defense.

Captain Anderson, in pursuance of his orders, immediately withdrew his force, avoiding the Hessian horse that made a weak pursuit, by taking a route across the fenced fields, and he recrossed the river in safety. On his march toward camp he met Washington's column marching in force to attack the enemy at Trenton. My grandfather was first addressed by Colonel Butler, then on the staff of the

commanding general, who expressed great
surprise that any one had dared to put
the enemy upon its guard, and, as an old
friend of the captain's hoped that he had
full warrant for his action. General
Washington then rode up, and was
greatly enraged upon learning where
Captain Anderson had been. He forth-
with sent for General Stephen, and demanded to know why his orders had
been disregarded, remarking: "You, sir,
may have ruined all my plans." General
Stephen assumed all responsibility and
stated that he had sent out the party to
obtain knowledge of the movements of
the enemy. General Washington dis-
missed Stephen to his station without
further words, and, in a calm and consid-
erate manner, directed Captain Anderson
to march his men in the vanguard, where
they would not be so greatly harrassed by

fatigue as they would be in their own place in the column.

This blunder of General Stephen's brought success to the American army. For Colonel Rahl, who had been warned of the projected movement, relaxed his vigilance when he learned that his dragoons had driven off the attacking party, and the soldiery gave themselves up to the festivities of the season. At eight o'clock of the next morning, twelve hours after the attack upon the picket guard, Washington won an easy victory from a surprised enemy.

Captain Anderson, in this second advance, received a wound in the hip from a yager ball, and was conveyed to Philadelphia upon a gun carriage. While lying in hospital in that city he was the victim of a severe case of small pox, the effect of which was not to improve his personal appearance.

The English writer, Gordon, who obtained his information relating to the first march upon Trenton from the Hessian lieutenant who commanded the picket guard, confuses my grandfather with Captain Washington, who was very active in the general engagement, and some other historians have followed him in the mistake. But that Captain Washington had no part in the *reconnoissance* we may be certain, for, in letters written from Trenton, upon the twenty-sixth of December, by General Washington and two others, no mention is made of this important affair, although his actual services are spoken of in detail. There are hundreds now alive who have heard my grandfather's comrades, around the hospitable table of Soldier's Retreat, speak of the part he took on that memorable Christmas night, and there are still some living who heard this matter discussed, when, in the autumn of 1817, James Monroe, president elect, visiting my grandfather at his home in Kentucky, met Andrew Jackson, Simon Kenton, and other men of mark. The information upon which this chapter is founded was was received from one who was present on that occasion. The Honorable Alfred Yaple, one of the Judges of the Superior Court of Cincinnati, a man learned in American history, informs me that he heard of Captain Anderson's skirmish with the Hessians from those who had it from General Arthur St. Clair, and that General St. Clair often said that my grandfather's conduct on that occasion gained for him Washington's friendship.

The Fortunes of War.

CAPTAIN ANDERSON served with the Fifth Virginia Regiment in the battles of Brandywine and Germantown. On the 10th day of February, 1778, he was promoted to be major in the First Virginia. With his new regiment my grandfather took part in the battle of Monmouth, in June of the last-mentioned year.

When, in the autumn of 1779, the Count D'Estaing undertook, with the aid of Lincoln's troops from Charleston, the reduction of Savannah, Major Anderson accompanied the expedition. As the

(24)

French commander was pressed for time, it was determined that the siege should be abandoned, and that an attempt should be made to take the place by assault. The attacking troops were ordered to advance with unloaded muskets. A British soldier, who, with fancied impunity, was picking off the officers of the Americans, was killed by my grandfather's black servant, Spruce, who did not consider that it was demanded of him to charge the enemy with an empty gun.

Major Anderson and some others had gained the parapet of the Spring Hill redoubt, when a Captain Tawes, with whom, when Tawes was a prisoner, my grandfather had lived on terms of intimacy, thrust his sword through Anderson's shoulder, and knocked him into the ditch; the fall giving him a hurt from which he never wholly recovered.

At the same moment, the British officer received his death wound.

The attack, though at several points successful, was, in the end, repulsed. Upon his way back to camp, my grandfather met Pulaski. The unhappy Pole was mounted upon a rough-moving pony, at whose every step the blood from a mortal wound churned up in the long boots of the rider. Until death released Pulaski from his sufferings, at some hour during that night, Major Anderson remained with him. He received from the dying man a sword, in memory of the sad service.

The continental forces were recalled to Charleston, where Major Anderson rejoined the Virginia line that had been sent down for the defense of that threatened point.

Here, nearly eighty years later, his son Robert, holding the like rank, was forced to yield up Fort Sumter to his fellow-citizens arrayed against his government.

Charleston was surrendered, when, by the regular approaches of a siege, the garrison was put at the mercy of the enemy; and Major Anderson remained a prisoner in the hands of the enemy for about nine months, suffering much hardship, often keeping off starvation with a few fish caught in the river bordering the camp; and the privilege of fishing was finally denied him.

Upon his release he joined General Morgan, who was about to withdraw before Lord Cornwallis. Major Anderson was so impressed with the military skill displayed in Morgan's movements on this retreat, that afterwards, when he had charge of Lafayette's rear-guard, he used the same tactics, and with like success, before the same enemy.

It was the custom of General Morgan,

after making the day's march, to go into
bivouac and build the usual fires. Then,
when his troops had taken supper, he
would withdraw them four or five miles,
and let them rest until morning. In this
way he avoided surprises, though followed
by one of the most wily and dashing
officers of the British service.

When Major Anderson reached Richmond he found an order from General
Washington directing him to report himself to General Lafayette, who had been
placed in command of the Continental
troops in Virginia, as it was supposed
that my grandfather's accurate knowledge of the country might prove of great
assistance to the Marquis in determining
his movements.

Mad Anthony Wayne.

IN the spring of 1781 Virginia was threatened by a hostile force of twenty-five hundred men, under the traitor Arnold, who was, however, superseded in the command by General Phillips before active operations were begun.

To the Marquis de Lafayette, with a few disheartened troops, was confided the defense of the colony. General Wayne had been directed by the commander-in-chief to march some detachments of Continental troops, that were at York in Pennsylvania, to the army of General

Greene in the Carolinas, and he had been further instructed to lend aid, while on his route, to Lafayette, provided the Marquis should demand it.

Lafayette was compelled to retreat from Richmond, closely pursued by the British forces, now increased to the number of seven thousand men by the troops of Cornwallis, and under the command of that active leader. The object of Lafayette's movement was to protect the stores that had been carried to Albemarle Court House and other points of present safety; while Cornwallis not only hoped to destroy these supplies that were of almost vital importance to the struggling colonies, but also believed that he might gain the whole of Virginia to the British arms.

Upon learning the nature of the orders given to General Wayne, the Marquis requested his immediate aid, and indicated to him the route his army would follow in its retreat and the point where the Pennsylvania troops should join it. Withdrawing now to this place of meeting, the Marquis exhibited to the enemy every proof of disorder and weakness. Cornwallis was confident that he had him in his grasp. "The boy can not escape me," wrote the Earl, joyfully anticipating the glory of depriving the rebels of one of their wisest advisers and ablest leaders.

This "boyhood" of Lafayette's was a matter of ridicule with the enemy and of indignant jealousy to the Continentals. Among these malcontents General Wayne was prominent, as well on account of his rank and reputation in the army as because his ardent temper made him most violent in the expression of his dissatisfaction.

The time fixed upon for the arrival of the Pennsylvania troops had passed by,

and yet nothing was heard from Wayne.
The delay of this officer, deferring the
forward movement, filled Lafayette's
mind with anxiety for the safety of Steu-
ben's detached force, and of the stores at
Albemarle. The Marquis, therefore, sent
Major Anderson to urge Wayne to
march with all haste, as the occasion
was a pressing one.

Major Anderson found General Wayne
in camp at a place called "The Red
House," and received from him an un-
gracious promise to move up. After the
expiration of three days, the Marquis,
having learned that Wayne was not ad-
vancing, again sent Major Anderson
with a peremptory order to join him by
forced marches, and Major Anderson
was instructed to remain with Wayne,
sending forward hourly dispatches to his
chief, until the troops should arrive at
the camp.

When Major Anderson reached Wayne on his second mission, he found that the General had moved but four miles from his former headquarters. Upon entering the room that served as the Adjutant's office, my grandfather saluted the General and his staff officers in a friendly and natural manner, and asking for pen, ink, and paper, sat down as if to write. Looking up to Wayne, whose curiosity had been aroused by this proceeding, he told the General that he had been sent by the Marquis de Lafayette to repeat the order for his advance, and that as he was about to forward the first of the hourly dispatches required of him, he desired to know what should be the nature of the report.

Wayne was at first amazed at the audacious intrusion, and staring at Major Anderson, asked, in a low tone, "Do you mean to insult me?" My grand·

father denied having any such intention,
but said that in the course of duty he carried the commands of a superior officer.
Wayne's voice, which had been husky
and choked with passion, now broke
forth like the thunder that has given a
low and threatening prelude: "Superior!
Superior! Do you dare call any damned
foreigner, and a boy, too, my superior?"
He then poured forth a torrent of oaths
and imprecations upon all foreigners, not
sparing my grandfather for having as-
sociated himself with "the fortune-
seeking Frenchman." He became more
vehement as he lashed himself into a
fury, and finally, in the rapidity of his
utterance, he fell into incoherent raving.
Nor did he cease from striding up and
down the room, stamping his foot in a
paroxysm of rage at each turning. It
was the indulgence in these furious out-

bursts of temper, and not his well-known
rashness in battle, that gave him the
nickname of Mad Anthony. At length,
fatigued by his violent action and the
force of his passion, Wayne gradually
subsided into human nature and even
into gentleness of manner. But any
reference to the object of Major Anderson's visit led to just such a scene as I
have described. Four times did he give
way to these frenzies, when, having re-
lapsed into a reasonable state of mind,
he joined the conversation, which one of
his officers had turned into a channel
that might divert his mind from the
dangerous topic. Wayne having expressed himself hopeful of a certain, but
perhaps distant, success for the American
arms, Major Anderson confessed that
his mind was filled with gloomy fore-
bodings. He was, as he secretly hoped

to be, pressed for his reasons. He
saw that the critical moment had ar-
rived, and with more words than were
customary with him he told the General that as the only hope of success
against a formidable foe lay in voluntary
union and subordination, the example he
had witnessed that day of an officer
high in rank and of distinguished services, refusing to obey the orders of a
superior, deprived him of the hope of a
useful or permanent success. "General
Wayne," said he, "I look to you to re-
move these apprehensions."

This condemnation of Wayne's course
seemed about to rouse his anger; but he
was, though jealous and excitable, a true
patriot and a real soldier, and with
almost that heat with which he had
lately refused to obey he cried out, "Tell
him I'll jine him! Tell him I'll jine

him! By God! tell him I'll jine him
to-morrow!"

[This incident was described by J. D. S., a
writer unknown to the author, in the *Richmond
Whig,* and his article was republished in the
Spirit of the Times. of October 22, 1843.]

At Yorktown.

GENERAL WAYNE brought only eight hundred muskets to Lafayette, but as there was need of prompt action, the Marquis boldly took the offensive. The faint-hearted Continentals caught the ardor of their young and gallant leader, and became eager to seek the glories that were to be won from a foe superior in numbers.

On several occasions Lafayette offered battle to the enemy, first taking care that he could retreat in case of need; but Lord Cornwallis refused his challenge in each case. Once, on the 5th of July,

(38)

Wayne rashly forced the enemy to turn,
and had not Lafayette been at hand, the
Pennsylvania regiments would have been
annihilated; for the British troops were
in strong force. Cornwallis was retiring
to some point on the coast, in obedience
to the orders of Sir Henry Clinton, in
order that his army might be available
for the defense of New York, should it
be required. This attempt to maintain
both New York and Virginia was made
against the better judgment of Cornwallis, and he had the mortification of
retiring with a larger force before the
advance of his despised opponent. When
the Earl had marched his men into the
peninsula, Lafayette saw that the enemy
was entrapped, and joyously wrote to
Washington, " It is the most beautiful
sight which I may ever behold."

Every effort was now made to insure
the capture of the embarrassed and en-

tangled army. The French fleet took
possession of the bay, and all of the un-
employed Continental troops were hur-
ried upon the scene. General Nelson
had been made governor of Virginia, in
view of such an occurrence, and the
militia promptly answered his call.

My grandfather had now been in the
military family of the Marquis de Lafayette for more than six months, and
had gained by his services and character
the confidence and friendship of his chief,
having on his part the greatest respect
and affection for the noble foreigner. It
was, therefore, a matter of sincere regret
to both that my grandfather was ordered,
about the first of September, to report to
Governor Nelson to assist him in or-
ganizing the militia. Upon the 19th
day of September, the third parallel of
approach having been opened, and all
hope of succor from Clinton having

been given up, Lord Cornwallis surrendered the place and the troops to the
allied armies.

During the whole of this campaign,
my grandfather's duties were of the
most arduous and responsible nature,
and so well were they performed that he
was rewarded by promotion to the grade
of Lieutenant-Colonel in the Continental
army, and he was at the same time appointed a Brigadier-General of Virginia
militia.

In April of the year 1783, the army
was disbanded, and Colonel Anderson
was with one voice chosen by his brother
officers surveyor-general of the lands
reserved to pay the Virginia Continental
line, and the selection was approved by
the State legislature.

The Frontier in 1783.

THERE were two districts reserved for
the troops of the Continental line.
One was a large tract of land in Kentucky, lying between the Green and
Cumberland rivers. The other was the
region lying between the Little Miami
and Scioto rivers, going back to the
headwaters of those streams in the Ohio
country. Hostile Indians inhabited this
latter district, and their frequent incur-
sions after game rendered Kentucky a
dangerous home for the pioneers.

My grandfather selected Louisville as
the most convenient place in which to es-

tablish himself, as it was midway between his districts. At the time he reached the frontier, in the spring of the year 1783, Louisville was nothing more than a few log houses scattered around the palisade work known as Fort Nelson, and in the territory that is now known as the State of Ohio there was not one permanent settlement.

In Kentucky, then a county of Virginia, the pioneers gathered for safety at the stations, going out to work the fields during the day, but coming in like sheep to the fold at nightfall.

These stations were simply huts connected by curtains of palisades, and sometimes huts only, pierced for musketry and placed so as to protect each other. From these primitive forts a few brave men would drive off an enemy of many times their own number. Indeed, it was seldom that a station was captured by the Indians unless through surprise or treachery, for the knowledge that no mercy could be expected from the savage foe nerved the pioneer's arm to a deadly aim, and he thought not of surrender.

As the surveyor-general my grandfather was compelled to remain almost constantly in his office, for assistants made the actual surveys and reported them to him. It is easy to imagine that the duties of these assistants led them into dangers and hardships. In small parties, and often singly, they would travel for hundreds of miles through Indian-haunted woods that never before had echoed to the step of a white man, dependent for their food upon the rifle and exposed to death in many forms. Of these men I mention the names of Generals Massie, Lytle, James Taylor, Duncan McArthur, and Lucas Sullivant, as some of the earlier appointments made by Colonel Anderson, and as those who have left their marks upon the times.

This office-life was not to my grandfather's liking, and, whenever he could lay aside his pen, he would seize his gun and seek the woods. In these excursions he was often accompanied by George Rogers Clark, the grandest actor on the scene, the founder of the Commonwealth of Kentucky, and the leader of one of the boldest expeditions in the history of war. These two would consider themselves happy when they could leave the safety of the fort, and without shelter, and exposed to many perils, wander in the grim forest.

In 1787 Colonel Anderson married a sister of General Clark's, and the next year he built a log house ten miles from Louisville, and with his wife, a babe, and some negro servants, moved into the wilderness.

Here my grandfather could gratify his
taste for the chase, but I doubt whether
the most fearless would consider "Soldier's Retreat," as he called his new
home, a very secure refuge. His nearest
neighbors, at Linn's Station, were five
miles off. In another direction, and but
a little further removed, lived Captain
Chenoweth and his family.

No record has been kept of the heed-
less travelers who fell victims to the
murderous red men of this region, but so
wary a backwoodsman as Colonel Linn
was killed by a wandering party of Indians within half a mile of my grandfather's house, and the fate of the Chen-
oweths I will hereafter relate.

A short time after Colonel Anderson
had taken possession of his home, a gentleman named Sales, and his negro man
Louis, were surprised and captured by a
small body of Indians. This party then

withdrew into the underbrush, and the
captives were directed to keep quiet.
Presently, one of the Indians gave a
shrill whistle, as if to call some one. At
the distance of a long rifle-shot Sales saw
my grandfather so intently following his
dog that the signal was not heard.
Again the Indian whistled, but, fortu-
nately Colonel Anderson disregarded it,
and walked off into safety. It was not
until the escape of Sales that my grandfather learned how narrowly he had
avoided the snare.

The Chenoweth Massacre.

ALTHOUGH the Indians had way-
laid many travelers, they had not
yet attacked any of the stations or houses
about Louisville, and, strange as it may
seem to us of this day, the pioneers lived
in fancied security. But an event of the
year 1789 showed them the dreadful dangers with which they had been threatened.

One night, in the year last mentioned,
my grandfather was awakened by hearing the suspicious sound of a moccasin-
covered foot upon the gravel-walk before
the house. Raising his right hand, he

cocked the rifle that lay loaded in the
rack above his head, and waited for the
next move of the supposed enemy. In a
moment there was a light tap at the door.
As it was a common trick of the Indians
to seek admittance into houses under
various pleas, my grandfather demanded
the name of his visitor. "I am John
Snow," said a familiar voice, "the Indians have attacked Chenoweth's, and I
alone have escaped." All that could be
learned from the frightened man was,
that while the family were at supper,
Captain Chenoweth being absent, the
savages had surrounded the house, and
that he had escaped by breaking through
their line.

A visitor, Mr. William Elliott, who
was sleeping in the room above the one
occupied by my grandfather, was called
down and sent to summon the men at
Linn's Station. Colonel Anderson at

once mounted a horse, and reached Chenoweth's as the day was dawning.

Upon the door-step was seated a little
girl of four years quietly playing with
her braided hair. She recognized my
grandfather as he rode up, and with a
calm voice, said, "We're all dead here,
Colonel Anderson."

Near the wood-pile at the side of the
house lay little Jamie, two years older
than his sister, with a deep wound from
a tomahawk in his forehead. To the surprise of my grandfather, he rose up and
seemed fully conscious. Jamie recovered, and I knew him when he was a
hale old man, seemingly none the worse
for this hurt, though the scar showed
that it had been a fearful one.

Mrs. Chenoweth was missing, but three
children and a servant were lying dead
upon the floor of the cabin, and the Indians had displaced and broken every

piece of furniture. The little girl who
was unhurt owed her safety to this de-
structive spirit, for she was in bed at the
time of the attack, and the Indians, in
pulling out the mattresses, had thrown
her down between the bed and the wall,
where she lay until they left the place.

When other neighbors came up, the
trail of Mrs. Chenoweth was taken, and
she was found, lying in the woods at no
great distance, nearly dead, her scalp
having been taken. She was given the
best care that those rude times afforded,
and was soon able to tell her sad story.

When the savages broke into the room
she fled through the open door, closely
pursued by one of them. At the moment he threw his tomahawk her foot
tripped and she fell, the weapon flying
harmlessly over her head. She lay there
motionless, and the Indian, thinking that
he had killed her, took out his knife,

and, cutting a circle about her head, tore off the scalp. Such was her fear that she did not cry out during the agony of that terrible operation. When he left her she was blinded with blood, and, as she was unable to rise, she had crawled to the place where she was found, in an effort to reach Soldier's Retreat.

For many years my grandfather did not see Mrs. Chenoweth, but when, on his journey to Virginia, he stopped at a wayside house, his first words drew out the exclamation : "Oh! Colonel Anderson," from a blind woman sitting in the room he had entered. It was Mrs. Chenoweth, who never forgot a sound she heard on that dreadful morning.

Time Flies.

WHEN, in the year 1793, General Wayne defeated the combined forces of the Indians at Fallen Timbers, a stop was put to the depredations of the savages, and the journey down the Ohio being comparatively safe, a great number of emigrants went to Kentucky, and the country about Soldier's Retreat became thickly settled.

The old log-cabin in which my grandfather had lived for several years gave place to a large and substantial house of stone, and there Colonel Anderson practiced a hospitality of the broadest kind.

To his table came all of his old army comrades who were passing up or down the river, the pioneers looking for homes, the wandering hunters, and even the Indians, who, a few years before, had waged relentless war against the white men, some of whom, perhaps, had lain in wait for their host. A gentleman told me that he had often met Little Turtle, who defeated General St. Clair, a harmless guest at Soldier's Retreat.

The new State flourished, and before the close of the century Colonel Anderson built a two-masted vessel, called the Caroline, which he loaded with the products of Kentucky and sent to London. Whether he gained anything by the venture I do not know, but a French clock that formed part of the return cargo is still keeping excellent time.

In 1797, his first wife having died two years before, Colonel Anderson married

Sarah, daughter of William and Ann McLeod Marshall.

With the beginning of the new century came a new order of things. Louisville was a city, and around Soldier's Retreat, where, a few years before, were dense woods and dreary canebrakes filled with wild beasts and savage men, were now smiling farms and peaceful friends. The people were no longer called upon to suffer hardships, for they were within the bounds of civilization, and the frontier had been removed further west.

Once again, in his seventy-fifth year, my grandfather revisited Virginia. What must have been his emotions upon re- turning as an old man to the scenes of his youth, after an unbroken absence of more than forty years.

Most truly and affectionately
Your old brother soldier
Lafayette

Friends Meet.

WHEN, after the lapse of nearly half a century, the Marquis de Lafayette came to see, in its strength, the nation that he had left in its infancy, he accepted the proffered hospitalities of Kentucky. A few days before his arrival in the State, my grandfather received the following note:

"*Colonel Anderson:*
" The committee appointed by the Governor, on the part of the State, to superintend the arrangements for the reception, and to provide for the accommodation of General Lafayette while on a visit

to this State, sensible of the worth of
your military services during our Revolutionary War, and knowing the public
relation in which you stood to him as
one of the aids-de-camp of that illustrious
man, beg leave, on behalf of the State,
to request that you will accompany the
General on his visit to Frankfort, and at
the public entertainment there to be
given him by the State.

"Your mo. obt. servts.,
"W. T. BARRY,
"J. BLEDSOE,
"THOS. BODLEY,
"C. S. TODD."

In accordance with the arranged order
of affairs, the Marquis, who came up the
river on a steamboat, was received by
the committee on the part of the State
at Louisville. I am under obligations to
Mr. J. F. D. Lanier, of New York City,
who was a witness of the scene, for the
following description of the meeting be-

tween the Marquis de Lafayette and Colonel Anderson :

"In the year 1825, General Lafayette made his first visit to the United States since the Revolutionary War had ended. I was then a citizen of the State of Indiana, and a resident of Madison. His travels throughout the length and breadth of the country were a grand ovation. He was received and welcomed everywhere, each city and town vying with the other in lavishing kindness, hospitality, and greetings to the 'nation's guest.'

"Among other places in the West he visited Louisville, Kentucky, which city was in the course of his journey from the South to visit Mr. Clay at Lexington. That was in the month of June of that year. He came up the Ohio river by steamboat, and landed at Shippingsport, a small town just below Louisville, that being the head of navigation of the Ohio river at that time. The boat that brought him up was expected to arrive at a certain hour of the day, and the whole country side were assembled on the banks awaiting his arrival. At length the boat appeared, and amid the wildest excitement and cheering approached the shore, where a plank was thrown out for the passengers to land, as was the custom of that day.

"Your grandfather, General Richard C. Anderson, who had served as one of General Lafayette's aids during the Revolution, together with your father, then a young man, were present on that occasion.

"It has afforded me, in after times, great pleasure to have been an eye-witness of the occurrence. Although fifty years and more have passed, still I have as vivid a recollection of the affair as if it occurred only last week.

"After the party had safely landed, General Lafayette, who was a little lame, and obliged to lean on a gentleman's arm by his side, surrounded by old friends, was

ascending slowly the steep bank of the
river, which was now covered with an im-
mense multitude, when, at once recog-
nizing your grandfather in the crowd,
whom he had not seen for forty years,
they rushed into each other's arms and
kissed each other!

"It was indeed an affecting scene, ever
to be remembered. It was with difficulty
that any one present could repress their
emotions at seeing the two friends, now
both well advanced in years, in each
other's embrace. I have a distinct recollection of the appearance of your grandfather on that day. His hair was white
as snow."

But after the old friends had recovered
from the shock at seeing in each other
how badly time had treated them, they
broke out into hearty laughter upon the
Marquis repeating the memorable words
of General Wayne: "Tell him I'll jine
him! Tell him I'll jine him! By God,
tell him I'll jine him to-morrow!"

Adieu.

ON the 16th day of October, 1826, atter a painful illness, borne with characteristic fortitude, my grandfather gave up this life, which, though passed in unceasing labor, and amidst great and constant perils, must be held to have been a happy one. He was at an early age inured to the hardships that the soldier and the pioneer must undergo, and he found pleasure in the excitements of the camp and of the border.

He was never rich, nor did he wish to accumulate money, but when the time came he found that he could afford to

give his children the best advantages in
their education. Though he never held
a political office, his career was a public
one, and he was thoroughly respected.

He lived long enough to see his children exhibit characters that promised to
reflect credit upon him. He had six
sons : Richard, who twice represented his
district in the National Congress, was
minister to the United States of Colum-
bia, and who died, greatly regretted, at
Carthagena, on his way to the Congress
at Panama, as Commissioner; Larz Anderson, of Cincinnati, lately deceased, a
scholar, and the conscientious steward
of his large fortune; Robert Anderson,
of Fort Sumter; William Marshall Anderson, one of the first to cross the
Rocky mountains, and who, when three
score years of age, made a scientific journey through Northern Mexico; John
Anderson, of Chillicothe, and Charles

Anderson, who made the speech before
the secession meeting at San Antonio, in
1861, in favor of sustaining the Union.